First published in 2006
by Hodder Children's Books

First published in paperback in 2007

Text and illustrations copyright © Mick Inkpen 2006

Hodder Children's Books
338 Euston Road, London NW1 3BH

Hodder Children's Books Australia
Level 17/207 Kent Street, Sydney NSW 2000

A catalogue record of this book is
available from the British Library.

ISBN: 978 0 340 91719 0
10 9 8 7 6 5 4 3 2

Printed in China
Colour reproduction by Dot Gradations Limited UK

Hodder Children's Books is a division of Hachette Children's Books
An Hachette Livre UK Company
www.hachettelivre.co.uk

Wibbly

Pig's Silly Big Bear

Hodder
Children's
Books

A division of Hachette Children's Books

Wibbly Pig
has a bear
so big,
he can hardly fit
on the page!

He eats his peas
one at a time.

It takes him ages!

Because, you see,
he cannot use
a spoon.

Yes, spoons mean
nothing to him.
  He eats his ice cream
with his paws,
and gets it

everywhere!

Wibbly's bear
does not
know how
to sit on
a potty,
or brush
his teeth,
or comb
his hair.

He scribbles
on the walls
and puts pyjamas
on his head.
He eats books.
He is hopeless
at hiding.

He can only count to one.
(And sometimes gets that wrong!)

So,

if this bear can't
even use a spoon
to eat his peas,
then please,
what is he
good for?

Well, he can jump!
And he can crash!
 And he can bash
his paws like
thunderclaps!

And he will whizz you
round and round
and up and down.
He is enthusiastic.
And you can climb up
on his back and pull
his ears.
And he doesn't
mind at all!

And if you whisper funny things to him he will **roar** with laughter.

And though he
cannot use a spoon
to eat his peas,
he will reach up
and grab the
moon
and bounce it
to you.

And he will be amazed

at the bubbles you blow for him.

And he will disappear
your trouble inside a

hug.

That's what he's good for.

And when
all your bubbles
have been blown
and blown away,
when Wibbly's bear
is no longer here,
when

he

is

gone...

. . . we will miss him
more than anyone.